THE HIGHLANDER WHO STOLE CHRISTMAS

ELIZA KNIGHT

KNIGHT
MEDIA

PRINCE CHARLIE'S ANGELS

The Rebel Wears Plaid
Truly Madly Plaid
You've Got Plaid

THE SUTHERLAND LEGACY

The Highlander's Gift
The Highlander's Quest
The Highlander's Stolen Bride
The Highlander's Hellion
The Highlander's Secret Vow
The Highlander's Enchantment

PIRATES OF BRITANNIA: DEVILS OF THE DEEP

Savage of the Sea
The Sea Devil
A Pirate's Bounty

THE THISTLES AND ROSES SERIES

Promise of a Knight
Eternally Bound
Breath from the Sea

THE HIGHLAND BOUND SERIES (EROTIC TIME-TRAVEL)

Behind the Plaid
Bared to the Laird
Dark Side of the Laird
Highlander's Touch
Highlander Undone
Highlander Unraveled

WICKED WOMEN

Her Desperate Gamble
Seducing the Sheriff
Kiss Me, Cowboy

HISTORICAL FICTION

Coming soon!

The Little Mayfair Bookshop

TALES FROM THE TUDOR COURT

My Lady Viper
Prisoner of the Queen

ANCIENT HISTORICAL FICTION

A Day of Fire: a novel of Pompeii
A Year of Ravens: a novel of Boudica's Rebellion

FRENCH REVOLUTION

Ribbons of Scarlet: a novel of the French Revolution

ABOUT THE BOOK

For eight months, Thane Shaw has patiently waited to enact his revenge against the Campbells, and finally he can't resist the opportunity that's presented itself: stealing their most precious treasure for his own—Lady Sarah.

NOTE TO READERS

Dear Reader,

I'm very excited to be a part of A Very Highland Holiday collection. My story, The Highlander Who Stole Christmas, is a fun tale loosely based on How the Grinch Stole Christmas by Dr. Suess. It's one of my very favorite Christmas stories, and I thought it would be a lot of fun to use some of the themes from it in writing this Highland holiday tale.

Thane is quite bitter when he heads down south from his clan's holding to Campbell lands where he plans to ruin their Christmas festivities and all of the holiday season by stealing Lady Sarah. But he may just find his heart growing by three, as did the Grinch.

While it's true that Christmas wasn't widely celebrated in the Highlands after being banned, and frowned upon even when the ban was lifted, there were some small pockets where traditions were maintained (probably in secret), perhaps a bit more quiet than how I portray celebrations in my story.

After all, it is said that the Christmas Carol, "O, Come All Ye Faithful" was written as a call to rebel arms after the birth of Bonnie Prince Charlie. How else would such a call be passed if rebels weren't singing in secret?

I wish you all a very merry holiday season, and a wonderful New Year.

Happy Highland Reading!
   XO,
   Eliza

To Andrea, because you always bring me Christmas cheer!

Revenge was a dish best served on a cold, snowy platter.

At least, that was what Laird Thane Shaw told himself as he headed out into the darkness just after nightfall, ignoring how the clouds covered the stars in the inky black sky. A blustery wind blew, and a man with less hate in his bones might have frozen to death. But his thirst for revenge was enough to keep him warm.

This was for his twin sister, Thea. If no one else felt the need to exact revenge on her behalf, then he would gladly take up the mantle. Thea deserved no less—in fact, she deserved so much more. Life, for one.

Damn his clan for fearing the wrath of the Campbells. The bloody bastards deserved to feel the same pain the Shaw clan endured. No matter their size, no matter their might, the Campbells couldn't get away with *murder*.

And he was going to teach them just that.

An eye for an eye—or rather, a sister for a sister.

Lady Sarah Campbell was about to become collateral

damage in a war waged between clans, and while he did feel a twinge of guilt at putting her life in danger for the sake of his bloodlust, at least he wasn't going to kill her. Unlike the Campbells who had violently stolen his sister's life.

And so, Thane ignored the warnings of the weather and rode out into the night before anyone could stop him.

Wrapped in his plaid to ward off the cold along with an extra riding blanket on his horse, Destiny, he rode over the moors. His horse's hooves knocked against the frozen, packed earth. White clouds puffed from his mouth and the horse's muzzle, and with each gust of wind, the ice on the tree limbs tinkled like musical wind chimes.

Eight long months had passed since the Battle of Culloden, which had not only changed the landscape of Scotland but the landscape of his clan. His entire life. And ended his sister's.

He'd been one of the lucky ones. Hell, if one could call him lucky. He felt cursed. Vexed with life, and guilt for surviving, when so many others had died for the cause. More than half of the Shaw warriors had been annihilated in battle. And those who'd made it were filled with such anguish and fear. Not to mention they'd had to hide from those who sought to kill them ever since. The Duke of Cumberland had orchestrated the catastrophic battle, and when it had ended, he'd put out the order for all Jacobite rebels to be murdered.

And still, Thane was here. But without his twin sister in the world, what more did he have to live for?

When he returned to his castle with Lady Sarah in tow, it would raise the morale of his people. Seeing that Thea's death was being avenged would bring them hope for a brighter future. Or in some way present a future that was less bleak. Even the dogs looked dejected these days. All of the clan's crops had been burned or stolen by dragoons, and what little stores they'd been able to hide were quickly dwindling. Neighboring clans were all in the same boat. The population itself was dwindling because of it, as some fled to the New World and parts of Europe. Escaping starvation, fear and grief.

At the very least, he might be able to extort some supplies from the Campbells when they came looking for Sarah. A ransom paid was better than a silly chit who required rations.

Lady Sarah Campbell...He'd not seen her since Thea had been wed to the Chief of Clan Campbell, but his memory of her was sharp. The lass had a confidence about her that came with the privilege of belonging to a powerful clan. One that had not seemed to fair as badly as the rest of the nation.

Trailing in undulating waves down her back and threaded with little white flowers, her red locks screamed out to the sun. Her lips were a perfect pink bow, accented by a beauty mark on the indentation of her creamy, dimpled cheek. But most noteworthy were her brown eyes, the kind that saw straight into a man's soul, disturbing him enough that he'd dreamt of them for months after their meeting.

What sort of things had a lass like that seen?

He hardly had to guess, given the brutality of her brothers. It crossed his mind then that perhaps Lady Sarah had witnessed his sister's death. A shudder passed through him, imagining what Thea had gone through. Why had their da arranged to marry her off? If Thane had been laird at the time, he'd not have agreed. But the responsibility had only fallen to his shoulders after the great battle, which had also stolen his da's life. And what was done was done.

Thane thrust aside those melancholy thoughts, or else he might guide his horse right off a cliff. Instead, he focused on his plan for infiltrating the Campbell stronghold and finding Lady Sarah as fast as he could.

Recognizing her was the least of his worries. Och, but Thane could pick her out of a crowd of a thousand fiery-headed beauties, of that he was certain.

What he worried about most was blending in with those in residence.

He planned to infiltrate the castle during their annual Christmas feast, which took place on the eve of the holiday, and steal her away while everyone was distracted by the celebration. Word had leached out across the Highlands that the Campbells still planned to celebrate despite the death and destruction that had hit their country. Another great blow to those who were still suffering.

Bloody bastards would be drunk on ale and wine and spiced cider, dining on the blood and guts of their peers.

The Campbells hardly suffered enough during the battle.

Of course, he knew that wasn't generous of him. All the clans had suffered. However, after learning that Thea had been left with little protection at the castle while the warriors had gone off to fight for Bonnie Prince Charlie and that when the ransom for Thea was demanded, the Campbells had refused, he wasn't feeling very charitable.

Oh, how his sister must have suffered at the hands of the butcher of the loyalist government army —also known as the Duke of Cumberland, son to King George who'd exacted his revenge on the Scottish rebels in favor of Bonnie Prince Charlie. Knowing that had made him harden his heart. Not just to the bloody *Sassenachs* who'd murdered her, but to those bastard Campbells, who might as well have been a party to it for they hadn't done much to protect her.

The place in his chest that used to burn a fire for a cause, had now frozen over, beating only for revenge.

BEFORE THIS MOMENT, LADY SARAH CAMPBELL HAD considered herself to be quite beloved by her family.

But now, as she backed against the wall in the darkened corridor, she realized what a complete fool she'd been. How easily she'd allowed herself to live in a bubble of pure fantasy. For it was evident now, considering the conversation happening on the other side of the tightly closed door, that she was only a commodity to be traded.

Her heart pounded in her ears, threatening to drown out the rest of the conversation happening within.

"There will be dozens of them present." This was the distinctive deep voice of her younger brother Edward.

"Ye were smart, brother, to invite everyone for the Christmas feast. No one will guess that we're actually brokering a deal." And that had been her other youngest brother Ellyson's reply.

Both her brothers chuckled, following by the sound of clinking. Were they giving cheers to selling her off?

Sarah fumed, hands fisted at her side, and her jaw clenched so tight she risked breaking a tooth. To them, she was a deal to be brokered, and neither of them seemed to care one wit that she was human, and until a few moments ago, their much-beloved sister.

Alas, that had all been in her mind, for it was evident now that she didn't mean as much to them as she thought she did. What an absolutely pathetic idiot she'd been.

The Christmas feast that she'd been helping to prepare for weeks—had in fact planned most of—was just a ruse to auction her off to the highest bidder. Why did they even bother with the feast to begin with? They could have saved themselves a lot of trouble and resources if they'd simply tossed her naked out into the moors for the quickest man to grab.

The clans were all hurting for money and staples since the Battle of Culloden, and though their clan was larger and richer than others, their size was the problem. They were large, *too large*, and had a lot of mouths to feed. So why not get rid of her and collect coin in the process?

She was nothing but a piece of property.

Jon was so busy with the rebellion these last few years that he'd put off arranging a marriage for her, and she'd been glad for it. Now that she was five and twenty, she thought for certain she'd be too long in the tooth for anyone to want her. Apparently not.

Sarah reached forward, preparing to bang on the door to tell them exactly what she thought of their disgusting plan, but what they said next stilled her.

"Northumberland's son will be there, as well."

"English bastards," cursed her brother Edward.

"Aye. We'll rob him blind if he's willing to take her."

Selling her to a bloody *Sassenach* made her stomach curdle, and she dropped her hand, pressing it to her gut, willing herself not to vomit. Northumberland…The same man who'd killed their brother and cousins on the field of battle.

Oh, dear God, she could not be wed to a *Sassenach*! Especially one who'd led a red-coated regiment against her own kin. What had got into her brothers?

Greed.

Sarah pinched her forearm, hoping this was a dream, but the pain radiating from the spot between her thumb and forefinger was very real.

They rattled off a few other names—all men she knew to be violent, and several more that were in league with the government, having gone against Bonnie Prince Charlie. Was that it then? After having fought for the prince at Culloden, her brothers were now prepared to sell their souls, and hers, to the highest bidder?

This wouldn't do. *It couldn't.*

Again, she raised her hand to rap on the door, to barge inside and tell them that they were crazy, but something stopped her. What if they denied her argument? What if they were so desperate for coin that they locked her up until the deed was done, the papers signed, and she was no longer a Campbell, but the wife of an Englishman?

Sarah backed away from the door, fear snaking its way down her spine. Her entire body started to tremble, and she bit her knuckles to keep from screaming.

There was so little she had control over. So little, indeed.

Except for one thing. Edward and Ellyson didn't need to know she was aware of their plans. If they weren't privy to her knowledge, and they continued with the charade of a festive Christmas celebration, they would have no idea that she was planning to escape, for that was what she must do.

Get as far away as possible.

Sarah would not wed any of the dozen or so men her brothers had invited into their home to steal her away. Never. And she wasn't against marriage—but she was against being sold to butchers.

She needed to escape, and perhaps the night of the feast was the perfect time. Her brothers would be so distracted sorting through the proposals, counting the coins that would soon line their coffers, they wouldn't notice she'd gone missing.

Blinded by tears, Sarah rushed back to her chamber and quietly shut the door. She leaned against the cool wood, sucking in a breath on a sob.

So much had changed in the last eight months. So much had changed in the last eight *minutes*.

This time last year, they'd been celebrating the holiday season with their clan. Singing, dancing. There had been so much hope for a better future with Jon as their new leader. Edward and Ellyson had been eager to join their comrades in the Jacobite rebellion, to bring honor to the clan. Their eldest brother Jon had been wooing his new wife, Thea.

Standing in the center of the great hall last Christmas, Sarah never would have guessed that she'd be where she was now. Jon and Thea dead. Her, escaping the family she'd once loved so fiercely.

Och, not once, but *still*. She loved them even now when they were tearing her apart on the inside.

Pushing away from the door, Sarah marched toward her wardrobe and wrenched it open. She pulled her leather traveling satchel out from behind the hanging gowns and stuffed her winter cloak inside, along with a gown, a pair of riding boots and a spare chemise. Then she opened the tiny box her father had carved for her and stared inside at the ring that had once belonged to her mother—the Campbell crest surrounded by rubies. It was her prized possession. If her brothers realized that she had it, they would steal it for certain.

But the ring had been given to her in private by her and Jon's mother just before she'd passed when she'd been barely five years old, and she doubted they were even aware of its existence. She put that into the satchel with her other belongings.

This was all she could take with her.

Where she would go, she'd not yet decided. Tonight, when it was dark, she would hide the satchel in the barn so that it was there when she was ready to leave. She prayed the feast tomorrow evening would give her some answers.

Until then, she'd need to come up with a plan—any plan, as long as she was gone before midnight struck on Christmas.

❧ 2 ❧

"Thanks for the borrow, sir. Though ye dinna know it yet, ye've done a great service to your fellow Scot." Thane gave a salute to the unconscious man at his feet, speaking as he divested the costumed Father Christmas from his garments and pulled them on himself.

He'd not had any idea of how he was going to sneak into Campbell castle until he'd happened upon the festively dressed man, and then he'd known exactly. Once inside, with Sarah held captive, he could divest himself of the costume and be about his business of abduction.

The old red velvet cloak smelled of must and horses, and other unmentionable things. Probably hadn't seen a wash since the Christmas before, but he tried not to think about that. Served these traitorous bastards right. They might have fought with the Scots on the field of battle, but Thane had to wonder if deep in their hearts, they were English loving all along.

Father Christmas was distinctly un-Scottish.

He tugged on the makeshift beard and curly, woolen hair

that had once been white but now was yellowed with age. Good lord, but it smelled like sour, not so well-preserved, ale.

Dressed, he hopped back onto Destiny's back and rode casually right through the gates, shouting messages of good tidings to those he passed and tossing little wrapped sweets that had been prepared for the occasion. All the while, in his mind, he recited a prayer for their traitorous deaths. The bastards.

In the bailey, a young lad came forward to take his mount by the reins. He was tall and lanky, hungry-looking. Eyes haunted. Poor bairn had likely been ill-treated by his clansmen.

"Och, wee laddie, I've a task for ye."

The lad cocked his head, interest in his eyes, especially when Thane passed him a coin.

"Rub him down, but then, if ye would, saddle him right back up again and keep him tied to the outside of the barn by the trough." Thane made an exaggerated look about the bailey teeming with people, some of whom appeared already to be quite into their cups. "I dinna think I'll be staying as long as I had anticipated." He gave a slow, exaggerated wink. "And if ye're a good lad, there's another coin where the first one came from."

"Och, Father Christmas, I'd do it for free." The lad beamed, looking as though the coin were the first that he'd ever seen, and likely the best gift he'd ever received in his entire life.

Thane regretted disappointing the lad when he found out who Thane truly was—the enemy. Would he trade the coin for Lady Sarah's life? Thane was willing to bet the lad would not.

Guilt ebbed at his conscience. But feeling sorry had no place in his plan, else he might as well walk right out the castle gates and back to where he came from. There was no time for regrets.

As Thane walked about the bailey, tossing out good cheer, sometimes through gritted teeth, he noted the various ways of escape and studied every female he passed in hopes of finding the red-haired beauty. The castle walls were being protected by guards. A good number of them, in fact, but they were all holding various cups likely filled with ale, wine or spirits, and they were all laughing and jesting instead of looking out over the snow-covered moors.

The winds had died down, and the massive bonfires in the bailey warmed the air. People danced and lazed about as if it were the height of summer rather than the middle of winter.

A tug at the bottom of his coat had Thane whirling about a little too exuberantly, afraid that he'd been caught. Much to his horror, the sudden movement sent a small child flying. The wee lass was sprawled on her backside, a look of alarm on her face. That expression alone was enough to make him want to abandon his cause. He'd not set out to frighten children. But her fear was quickly erased when she spied his beard and velvet coat. A tentative smile curved her tiny mouth.

Thane rushed forward, extending his hand. "My dear, I am so verra sorry."

The wee lass grasped onto his outstretched hand with wide, blameless eyes.

Forcing a smile, he said, "Why do ye no' tell this clumsy Father Christmas what it is ye wish for."

The bairn stood before him, blinking upward with large eyes, hands clasped in front of her, and without preamble said, "I wish to have our lady and laird back."

The lass could not have done more damage if she'd thrust a dagger into the center of Thane's heart. Her request broke his heart, and he found it hard to breathe for a moment. What innocence...

"Lady Thea was helping my ma with the new bairn in her belly. 'Tis being quite troublesome. And the laird, my da said he was twice the laird as these new ones. Says only the weak need to rule together." Truth out of the mouths of bairns.

Thane choked on his heart, which seemed to have removed itself from his chest and thrust its way up into his throat. He, too, had thought it odd that Edward and Ellyson Campbell had made a pact to share the lairdship.

He swallowed and then patted the lass on the head. "How old are ye?"

"Six summers."

"Well then, ye're practically grown. I bet ye can be a great help to your ma with the bairn."

The lass beamed up at him. "I think I can. But..." She shook her head and bit her lip. "What if she doesna want my help?" The wee thing looked so worried.

Thane knelt before her at eye level. "All mothers want help from their older bairns with the younger set. Trust me."

The lass held her hands to her chest, a beaming smile cutting across her face. "Oh, thank ye, Father Christmas. Ye've given me a great gift."

She hugged him tightly, her little arms barely reaching around his middle, and Thane awkwardly patted her back.

"Go on now, afore ye're missed."

She skipped off, and again he felt that perhaps his plan had been misguided. The wee lass missed Thea.

God, he missed his amazing sister too.

And that was why he needed to avenge her death. He was not the only one suffering from Thea's loss—the people were missing their mistress, their healer.

A tap on his shoulder had him startling once more. He

turned around a bit more carefully to avoid knocking down someone else. Only this time, he found himself staring into a pair of inquisitive brown eyes, with an equally inquisitive pair of red arched brows.

"A word, Father Christmas?" Her voice was low and silky as she made her request.

Finding Lady Sarah Campbell had been a lot simpler than he thought, for she had been the one to locate him.

❧

SARAH HELD HER SHOCK IN WELL BY MASKING IT WITH curiosity.

Just what was Thane Shaw doing here, and dressed as Father Christmas of all things?

The man had a death wish to be certain, for why else would he appear here, apparently unarmed and unaided? She glanced around surreptitiously. No one seemed to recognize him just yet, but that didn't mean they wouldn't soon. His face was quite distinctive. Blue eyes that were flickering in the bonfire light, the same shade as Thea's. His golden locks were hidden beneath the decrepit wig, but she'd bet all the grain in the storehouse that it was him.

"Is that your wish, my lady? I'm only giving away one to each soul."

She rolled her eyes. "Ye dinna seem to grasp just what your position here is, sir."

"Father Christmas," he insisted.

"As ye say." Miraculously, she kept from rolling her eyes at him.

"Is over there fine?" He indicated the barn. "Ye can tell me what ye would rather see as my position."

He handed her a sweet from his satchel, but she pushed it back. "Nay, thank ye."

Thane held out his arm to her. She considered arguing about going toward the barn with the man, but then she realized perhaps now was the exact moment she needed to make her move. No one would care if they saw her walking about with Father Christmas. She might easily be able to slip away with him as a distraction.

Besides, she had to find out just what the devil he was doing here.

The soft velvet of the red coat was straining from the breadth of his muscular arms, and she wouldn't be surprised if, at any moment, there was a tearing sound as his body gained its freedom from the restrictive garment. Normally a red coat would scare the devil out of everyone, fearing for their lives that the dragoons were back and ready to murder them all. Father Christmas was the only one who could get away with it. But Thane Shaw was *not* the man she'd hired to play the part.

At the barn, she let her hand drop, and when he faced her fully, his thoughts shuttered from his face.

"I am ready for my lesson." There was a teasing note to his words that she found surprising, given the intensity of how much she knew he disliked her family. That had been evident at Thea and Jon's wedding, and even more so after her death.

"Father Christmas doesna grant wishes to souls," Sarah mused. "Ye're confusing too many ideologies."

Thane wiped his hand down the neck of a sleek black horse that did not belong to the Campbell clan. She guessed it was his, judging from the familiar way he stroked the mane.

"He's a beauty," she said, adding her hand to the mix. "My

brother had one just like it. Though truth be told the horse preferred his wife."

He stiffened beside her, catching on that she spoke of Thea. Oh, how she missed her. Wanted to talk to Thane about his sister, but knew that broaching the subject now when he was trying for anonymity would likely be the wrong course of action. Then again, if she was going to get what she wanted, there was no time like the present.

"What is it ye wished to speak to me about?" he asked.

"I know who ye are."

"Then ye must know why I've come."

"I have an idea, but I dinna think it will work," she said.

His gaze met hers, steel blue. "Just what is it ye think I'm here to do?"

"Lay siege." She shrugged. "Some sort of revenge."

"Ye have the latter right, but I'm afraid ye've got the execution wrong."

The way he said "execution" with a bite to it had her flinching. Was that what he thought had happened to Thea? No doubt.

"I dinna deny that our clan likely is in need of some sort of punishment for what happened to your sister, but if ye should die too, ye will be of no help to your people."

"I think ye're wrong," he said, a menacing undertone. "I think what I've got planned will be a massive help."

Sarah sighed. "What is it ye have planned then?"

He winged a brow in challenge. "Climb onto my horse, and I'll tell ye all about it."

"Climb onto your horse?" She let out a short laugh and narrowed her gaze, the realization of his plot dawning. "Ah, so ye wish to abduct me."

He pressed his hand to his chest. "That is *my* Christmas wish."

Sarah sucked in a heady breath. Here was a gift placed right before her. The means to her escape. And he had no idea. They could kill two birds with one stone. He'd get his revenge, and she'd get her freedom.

She didn't even bother putting up a fight. "Can I get something from the barn first?"

Thane looked taken aback. "As I'm certain ye've no' been abducted before, I feel obliged to let ye know that will no' be possible."

Sarah leaned in close enough that she could smell the stink of the rotting wool beard. "But, you see, I have already packed a bag."

"What?" he sounded exasperated.

"I..." She licked her lips. "I was going to run away."

"Why?"

She glanced around, wondering if anyone had taken note of just how long she'd been talking with Father Christmas, but everyone was enjoying the drinks and food and paid them no attention. At least not yet.

"My brothers have arranged for several men to make offers for my hand this evening. One of whom is English. Nay, thank ye."

Thane groaned. "Fine. Get your bag, but I'm coming with ye. And just so we're clear, this is still me taking ye, no' me saving ye."

"Aye, of course," she nodded emphatically, grateful he was letting her get the satchel.

❧

THEY ENTERED THE BARN, AND SHE SPOKE TO THE SAME wee lad Thane had given a coin to. "Just getting a sack of gifts for Father Christmas," she explained.

Thane tossed the lad another coin, which quickly distracted him from their task.

A second later, she emerged with the satchel, beaming a smile at the lad and avoiding eye contact with Thane.

"Here we are. Thank ye, Georgie, for all ye've done with the horses tonight. I know it's been quite an ordeal with Harry sick."

The lad blushed and kicked at the barn floor. "Thank ye, my lady. I'm more than happy to help."

The lad glanced down at the coin in his hand, and Thane could practically see the thoughts about what he'd spend it on popping from his mind.

Outside of the barn, Thane took Sarah's satchel and attached it to his saddle.

"Wait." She touched his arm, and he ignored the frisson of heat that shot through him. "I need my cloak so that no one will see me."

This was ludicrous. She was actually helping him abduct her. This chore could not have been any easier. He was a little disappointed.

"Good idea." With his mount blocking him from the crowd in the bailey, he tossed the beard and wig, took off the red jacket, hanging it on the trough and then put on his own cloak.

A few minutes later, they were riding outside of the gates with no one the wiser that Father Christmas had just stolen the best prize of all.

3

Though the snowfall had ebbed before Thane arrived on Campbell lands, the storm had steadily picked up since they'd ridden away the night before. Save for a few short breaks to rest Destiny and relieve themselves, they'd ridden through the night. At times Sarah was alert, leaning away from him, and at other times her body sagged against him.

He'd pulled her onto his lap and given her the extra blanket he had, and she'd buried herself inside of it so much that he could barely see her. If not for the weight of her body against him and the unintelligible words he could hear her murmur in her sleep, he might not have known she was even there.

They were at least another day's ride from his holding south of Inverness, but with exhaustion setting in along with the renewed storm on this Christmas morning, they had nothing for it save to stop at the same place he'd stayed the night before on his way to Campbell lands—Balthazar's.

Good God, it had been a mess...But at least no one would come looking for them there.

All through the night with Sarah on his lap, he'd followed the same northern star, keeping him on the right path. The lass had been quiet, thankfully, because he'd not wanted to talk, but rather concentrate on the horrible weather and the road ahead. Not to mention any sounds from behind them.

If no one had realized she was gone the night before, they'd certainly be noticing now with the sun rising on the horizon. Christmas morning, the lass would have been expected to wed, or at the very least, woken in her own bed and joined her clan for breakfast.

Knowing that he had many hours lead and the storm to protect them, a stopover at Balthazar's, though it seemed a risky move, would not be as dangerous for them.

"Are ye awake, lass?" he asked.

She stirred in his arms, stretching her arms out and then tucking herself quickly back into the blanket. "Aye. Where are we?"

Thane glanced toward the smoke curling into the sky just ahead, his stomach souring. This was the last place he wanted to be. Well, not the last—that would be Campbells's dungeon. "Balthazar's Tavern."

"Well, this will be a new Christmas adventure." There was a bit of excitement in her tone that he found alarming.

"Nay, lass. 'Tis no' that kind of place. We'll need to be on our guard. Dinna mention your name," he warned. "And I'm no' a Shaw while we're here, and ye're no' a Campbell, understand?"

Sarah stiffened in his arms. "Who might ye be, then?"

"Munros. Headed home from the clan wedding of our cousins near Lindsay lands."

"All right...Is there a reason ye've named clans who fought with the dragoons at Culloden?" She sat up a little farther, her bottom rubbing against his thighs.

Thane groaned at her movement. "Aye, we're headed into the snake pit."

"Oh," she breathed out, the excitement gone from her voice. There was a long pause, and he could practically hear the questions racking up in her mind. "And are we brother and sister for this journey?"

"Nay." He clamped his mouth closed, shifting a little farther back on his saddle. "Ye're my wife. Then none of the bastards will see fit to mess with ye."

"That kind of a crowd, eh?"

"The patrons of Balthazar's fought on the other side of the battlefield, lass. And they are no'...friends of ours. They are rough about the edges. But stick with me, and ye'll be safe."

"Oh." There was fear and sadness in her sigh.

"We'll stay only as long as the weather demands," he said.

She nodded, the top of her head tapping against his chin, nearly making him bite his tongue. The snake pit was going to be a reprieve away from this temptress. She didn't even realize how much she was...*bothering* him. Perhaps it was just that it had been so long since he'd been with a woman. Not that he found the adventurous lass in his lap to be of any interest at all.

"'Tis there." He indicated the tavern just a stone's throw away to get his mind off her squirming, enticing body.

The tavern was built of thick, heavy stones. Tiny windows barely emitted any candlelight now that it was morning, but come night, the wee squares of light would lure in weary travelers.

The thatched roof was covered in thick snow, and Thane wondered how long it would take before a part of it collapsed in on the inhabitants. Given the state of the inside, he'd hazard to guess very soon.

Thane led Destiny on a path that had been recently cleared around the back of the tavern to where the stable was located. A young lad stood in the doorway, rubbing his hands together. A shovel leaned on the side of the stone building beside him. Clearly, he was the one who had shoveled the path. Another lad shoved him aside with an armload of wood. They'd have a nice fire going on inside to keep themselves and the horses warm. A small curl of smoke leached from the ceiling, which was good. At least they'd managed to keep the chimney clear.

"Got room for another?" Thane called.

The lad nodded and hopped forward on feet that were probably frozen. He reached for the reins, holding tight while they dismounted, each of them grabbing their respective satchels.

"Gonna cost ye, but Balthazar will collect inside," the lad said, teeth chattering.

"Thanks, lad." Thane reached into his sporran and pulled out a coin. "For ye and the others in the stables. Keep my mount well."

"Aye, sir. Thank ye." The lad led Destiny inside, telling him exuberantly how much oats he was about to have for his breakfast. He called over his shoulder, "Ye can go in the door to the kitchens rather than trudge about."

"Thank ye." He took Sarah by the hand. Her fingers were small, slim and freezing. "Goodness, ye should have told me how cold ye were."

"No' my place to complain, though, is it?"

Saints, did she really think he meant to torture her on top of the abduction? "'Tis no' complaining. I dinna want ye to lose a finger."

"Ye dinna?" She glanced up at him, and he could figure out

the rest of what she meant, that a finger was a lot smaller of a thing to lose than one's life.

The truth was he didn't want her to lose a finger—not even a hair on her head.

"Remember what we discussed," Thane said gruffly. "Munros on the way back from Lindsey lands."

"I'll no' forget." She shuddered, and he had a feeling it was not from the cold.

THE KITCHENS WERE SMOKY AND FILLED WITH SHOUTED orders as scullions rushed to follow the head cook's demands. It smelled enticing, rich with herbs and baking scones. There was a savory scent that belied the large pot of porridge being ladled into bowls from the hearth fire. All of the aromas reminded Sarah how little she'd eaten in the last few days, since she'd been so worried about the Christmas Eve celebration and subsequent auction of her life.

Thane had offered her nothing but a canteen of water on their ride here, and she hadn't asked for more. It had been the middle of the night, after all, and he wasn't responsible for her having missed supper. Besides, she'd spent most of the time sleeping, keeping warm and trying to refrain from annoying him so he wouldn't change his mind and take her back to her brothers.

"Get out, ye rapscallions!" shouted the cook, swinging a ladle in their direction. A few speckles of porridge hit Sarah's cheeks. "Food will come when 'tis good and ready."

Thane ducked the swinging utensil, and the second fling of oats. Barely having time to wipe her face, Sarah followed suit, rushing from the kitchens. However, they went the wrong way and ended up in the scullery room, where they were met by a buxom redhead who greeted them with a saucy grin, her hands buried in a wash bin full of dishes.

"Och, but ye'll no' be doing your dirty business in here, ye two." She pointed toward the door, droplets of water flinging in their direction. "Back to the common room with ye."

Sarah's face heated, and she was sure it flamed as red as her own hair at what the woman suggest with that line about "dirty business." She might not be as worldly as some, but she knew exactly what that referenced.

"We got turned around," Thane explained. "We just arrived and came in the back door."

The irritation dissipated from the woman's face. "Well, in that case, welcome to Balthazar's. He's my da. I'm Carrie, and this is our tavern. Will ye be taking a room?"

"Aye, that would be verra much appreciated," Thane said.

"Of course, I'm just back here helping out while I waited for my own room to be tidied up after it was let out to someone else." The woman narrowed her eyes, wet, red hands on her hips. "Ye wouldna be here causin' trouble, would ye? We've had a few troublemakers about the past fortnight or so."

"Oh, nay," they both answered at the same time. Then as if they'd been playing this game for more than a few minutes, they glanced at each other and laughed like two lovebirds.

"Sorry," Sarah said with a giggle. "Newlyweds. I'm S— Samantha Lindsey, I mean Samantha Munro now. This is my husband—Tobias Munro."

"Och, I see. Welcome, welcome and congratulations. Ye'll have a round of ale on us, I'll see to that. Go on out to the common room, and in the meantime, I'll have a room set up. Oh," she squealed. "And one more thing. I've go' a special room here, my Chamber of Sorrow, if ye'd like to pay respects to anyone that ye lost in the battle. Doesna matter the side. We all lost that day."

Carrie had a whole chamber devoted to prayer for the dead Scots and traitorous dragoons? Immediately she wondered if anything belonging to her brother would be in that room.

It was a mighty task to hide her horror, but Sarah managed it. "Thank ye kindly, Carrie. I'm sure we'd love to enjoy it later today."

"Excellent. Now go on with ye. Cook is going to begin serving soon, and if ye miss out on the meal, it will be a while before supper."

Carrie ushered them out of the scullery through the kitchen, where this time they dodged scraps of cabbage tossed their way and finally made it into the common room. The tiny windows barely let in any light, and the ceiling was low. The floors were made of dirt, strewn with straw, which was a shock to Sarah, given the only taverns she'd ever been in had either wood or slate flooring. What were they trying to hide beneath the straw? But she needn't have wondered, for the stench in the commons quickly dispelled the delicious scents from the kitchen. It smelled like...

Dog excrement.

Sarah tried not to gag at the overpowering smell. She glanced up at Thane to see if he'd noticed, but he was busy scanning the patrons and available tables. Several dogs lounged by the hearth sleeping, but there was one who'd taken up the telltale curved back pose of disposing of his bowels.

"Dear God," Thane muttered to her under his breath. "We'll take our meal in a chamber. Hopefully, the private rooms are better."

"Good idea." She leaned closer to him as if that would somehow make her feel better.

A large, bald, older man slapped his hand on a table with a friend, shouting for the dog to cease his business, before addressing them. "Welcome, newcomers. I'm Balthazar."

His beard looked similar to the fake one Thane had been sporting at Campbell castle, and if she had to guess, Sarah thought it probably smelled worse.

"Thank ye, sir. We're waiting on a room your daughter is having prepared for us," Thane said. "And if we could have our meals served there? Newlyweds." He added a wink for emphasis, which got a round of cheers from those in residence and started the hounds to howling.

Sarah was not against dogs; she loved them dearly. Her own sweet Mildred had just passed the month before. But these hounds were unruly, and she guessed it had something to do with the tavern owner himself, who seemed something of a wild man.

"Come, come. I've got one already set up." Balthazar ushered them through a series of chambers. "Will this do?"

But before they could reply, Carrie shouted, "Da, I've got another one prepared for the newlyweds."

She took them to a door across from the one her father had suggested. Before opening it, she leaned in a little close, speaking conspiratorially. "On the other side of this wall is my Chamber of Sorrow." Carrie glanced down at her feet, then back up at them brightly with her green eyes. "I'm hoping the souls whose possessions I've got displayed there will bless your union. And that it will bring me good luck in finding my own gentleman husband."

And what type of gentleman would that be—an English dragoon or a Jacobite rebel? Somehow, she managed to mask her musings and offer her thanks enthusiastically.

"Gave ye the best bed in the tavern. Sheets have been cleaned recently. Dinna mind about the table, it will make do."

As soon as Carrie and Balthazar shut the door behind them, Sarah turned to Thane. His handsome features were masked with indifference, but then his brooding gaze latched onto hers.

Mildly teasing, but partly serious, Sarah said, "Just where in blazes have ye brought me, sir? I promised to behave. Ye need no' have added torture to your abduction."

Thane raised his brows, arms crossing over the wide expanse of his muscled chest. "I could leave ye here. Maybe Cook will stop swinging her ladle long enough to offer ye a position?"

4

Sarah laughed. "Were ye sotted on your last sojourn? Or is this what I should expect of the Shaw holding?"

Thane grunted, smirking at her joke, before quickly wiping away his mirth. They were supposed to be enemies. They *were* enemies. He'd abducted her, even if she had come willingly.

"I wish I could say I was, and no, Shaw is an oasis of calm," he drawled, turning his gaze to their private hell. The chamber was not as unwelcoming as the common area of the tavern, and Thane was more than happy to take it for the night. Hopefully, that was all they would need it for.

"Ha! I'll believe that when I see it!"

Though this floor was also dirt-packed, a carpet that appeared recently beaten lay on the floor beside the bed, which was shoved against a wall.

The wooden bed frame sagged from the lumpy straw mattress that appeared to weigh an unfathomably vast amount, and tossed on top of it was a plain wool blanket. At least it did look clean, as Carrie had said. She and her father seemed like they aimed to please. If he'd been on better terms with them, perhaps a regular, Thane might have told them a simple redecorating of the main tavern room would bring in more guests. But they seemed smart enough to have figured that out on their own, which meant they probably purposefully kept it...*rustic*.

Two stools flanked a small table that was missing half a leg, but an upside-down bucket had been placed to steady it. Best rented chamber in the place—that was saying a lot. He kind of wished that Balthazar had opened the other chamber door, so he'd have something to compare it to.

Perhaps there was a certain charm in providing such a medieval tavern to those looking to go back in time. A time when Scotland had not been trampled over by dragoons. Saints, but he could not remember such a time ever having existed.

Thane turned away from the bed to investigate a crumbling iron brazier that had seen better days. The room was chilly and could do with a bit of heat. He picked up the poker resting on the rim and jabbed at the half-burned logs in the cavern. One of them crumbled to ash, sending up a plumb of dust, which had them both waving in front of their faces and coughing.

"I'm no' that cold," Sarah said with a cough and a laugh.

Thane groaned and dropped the poker. "Good. I'm afraid if I light it, the whole room will blaze."

"It might go to flame anyhow with the way it was roaring in the kitchen and the common room." She giggled and backed away from the brazier. Either she was daft, or she was the type of person who always seemed to look on the bright side of the coin. While he wanted to think it was the former, he was fairly certain it was the latter, which only ended up endearing her to him.

"I hardly noticed," he quipped. "Though I did wonder if

ye were going to lick the oats off your face."

"Ha! Maybe I should have, for I am starving." Sarah tossed her satchel onto the bed, and surprisingly a plume of dust did not rise with it.

Carrie had not fibbed about cleaning the bedding. Well, that boded well for their sleep. Och, but they would have to share a bed. There was barely even any room on the floor for Sarah to curl up on, and he wasn't going to make her sleep on the dirt-packed earth, despite there being a rug tossed down.

Sarah pulled out one of the stools and sat on it, wobbling a little and catching herself on the uneven table, nearly dislodging the bucket. "Whoa," she said, finally managing to catch her balance.

This only seemed to make her laugh, and Thane couldn't help but notice her dimple and the beauty mark that winked in and out with her humor.

She was beautiful, and it wasn't fair. Under the circumstances, he should not find her so attractive and fascinating. Instead of taking the stool opposite her, Thane leaned against the door, arms crossed, one ankle over the other, and stared in her direction. He told himself he was doing as an abductor would, but truly, it was to put distance between them because the way she was wriggling her bottom on that stool reminded him all too well of their journey on Destiny.

Sarah cocked her head, a tease in her dark eyes. She stared back at him, a bit of humor dancing about her mouth too. "Goodness, but ye sure are brooding. If ye're doing that for my benefit so that I remember ye're my captor, I assure ye, I am well aware, and I dinna plan to go anywhere."

A knock vibrated the door at his back, and Thane pushed away from it, opening it to see who would interrupt them.

Carrie stood in the hallway with a tray of food, and one of the lads from the stable behind her held a jug and two cups.

"We've brought your breakfast, a bit standard for us, but I assure ye supper will be delightful. And we've got a mid-morning Christmas treat too. Are ye planning to dine in your chamber this evening as well?"

"Aye." Thane's mouth watered at the simple fair. Lord, but he was starving. If he recalled correctly, the butter here last time was surprisingly good.

"All right, good then. When ye finish, if ye like, I can show ye the Chamber of Sorrow." Carrie beamed a smile at them and shifted on her feet.

"Hmm," Thane said. "We'll consider it."

Sarah was beside him then, her hand on his arm. "We'd love to see it. Perhaps with a bit of food, my husband will be more cheerful." She nudged him in the elbow as if she were the one in charge of their current circumstances.

Thane raised a brow and forced a smile that appeared genuine. "I do apologize. I'm starved, and I tend to get a bit grouchy when I'm hungry," he explained.

"Och, dinna we all," Carrie said with a laugh. She pushed past them into their chamber and placed the tray of food on the table, then took the jug and cups from the lad. "Feel free to leave the tray on the floor outside the chamber when ye're done. The lads will come by soon to collect it."

When Carrie had left, Thane shut the door and stared at Sarah, who was pouring ale into the cups and setting out the food.

"Why are ye being so agreeable?" he asked. "I abducted ye. I am dangerous."

❧

SARAH GLANCED UP FROM WHERE SHE'D PLACED A SPOON IN Thane's porridge, beside the melting ball of butter.

"Why are ye dangerous?" she asked, studying him from head to toe. He was large; there was no doubt. Tall and muscular, where his sister had been small. A few faint scars, and a nose that had been broken more than once, showed he was a warrior, and the mere fact that he was still alive was proof he could handle himself. But that didn't frighten her. If anything, it made her feel safe.

Mayhap she was mad. For he did have a point.

He stalked forward, the way a predator hunted prey.

Instead of being scared, she found herself wanting to meet him halfway. Mayhap they weren't getting enough air in this chamber.

"Your family is responsible for Thea's death."

Sarah nodded. She'd been waiting for him to say those words. They gave her something else to focus on besides the way her heart was beating wildly against her ribs. "Come, let's eat while we talk."

The way he grimaced, she thought he would disagree, and her stomach growled in protest, but he did come forward and take the stool opposite the one she'd claimed.

"Thea was—" she started, but he interrupted her.

"How dare ye say her name?" He stabbed his spoon into the nearly melted butter.

"She was my friend." Sarah boldly met his gaze. "My brother, Jon, loved her."

Pain flickered in Thane's eyes, and doubt. He likely didn't know whether or not he could believe her, and she understood why.

Sarah swirled the golden, dissolving lump of butter around her porridge. "I loved her, too. She brought life to our clan. Added light where there was darkness. Jon had been so disparaged by what was happening in Scotland—we all were—but she gave him hope."

She put down her spoon, suddenly unable to take a bite. Instead, she took a sip of bitter ale.

Thane did the same, gulping the entire contents of his cup and then refilling it. "What happened?"

The fact that he asked her that showed he expected to hear the truth from her, and she was more than willing to give it.

"I might be a traitor to Edward and Ellyson for telling ye this, Thane, but I dinna believe that I'd be betraying Jon, or Thea or our clan for that matter. After we lost Jon at the Battle of Culloden, my brothers...they decided to rule the clan together. One in charge of the common people and one in charge of our soldiers." Here she paused. "But it started even before then. They were always arguing with Jon over edicts he'd implemented or new ways of doing things. They hated that Thea was beloved by the clan, that a lot of the changes happening had started with her. She was brilliant, but ye know that. Edward and Ellyson were jealous, really."

This was the part that Sarah didn't want to talk about, but she knew she had to tell him. He needed to understand that what happened to Thea was not on the entire clans' heads.

"They were increasingly hard on her after Jon died. Worried, I think, that she might be with child and that child would eventually take the place they'd claimed. So, when Thea was taken by the dragoons while gathering various herbs and roots just outside the castle walls, they declined to pay the ransom. They thought it better to be rid of her." Sarah shook her head. "I pleaded with them, but they refused. I dinna think they believed she'd be killed, just taken away and married off to some English general."

"But she *was* killed." Thane's voice was low and fueled by anger and pain.

She reached for his hand then but pulled back at the way

he curled his fingers into the wood of the table. Comfort from her could come in the form of truth, but not yet from touch. That was the more appropriate form, anyhow.

"Aye. Right in front of us as we stood on the battlements." Sarah choked on a sob, bringing her hands to her mouth. "She didna deserve it. There was no retaliation. And I waited every day for ye to come and avenge her. I would have given ye the keys to the castle if ye'd asked."

Thane's anger shifted to suffering. "And that is why ye came so willingly? Because ye think ye deserve to bear the brunt of whatever revenge I've got planned?"

Sarah shook her head, shifted forward in her chair and then locked her gaze on his. "I told ye they were selling me off to the highest bidder."

"And ye think ye might have suffered Thea's fate."

She shrugged. "I could have."

He was quiet a long time, staring into his porridge as he slowly spun his cup of ale on the table. Time ticked silently for so long she worried that he wasn't going to speak again. Sarah sat on the edge of her seat, willing him to speak, to at least look up. He had to believe her.

When he finally did, his voice was tight with emotion. "I dinna place blame on ye, Sarah. But knowing what ye've told me, it would be impossible for me no' to bring war to your clan."

This she knew, but she was desperate to find a way out of it. To protect her people, even if her brothers wouldn't. "If I could beg ye no' to...If there were some way to punish Edward and Ellyson for what they've done without bringing pain to the people. They loved Thea, and she loved them."

Thane's eyes were hard, the line of his mouth unbending. "I canna see a way out of it."

5

Thane was torn.

He'd known already that his sister had suffered. The vague and unemotional missive that he'd received after her death from the new lairds of Campbell had been terse and to the point. Over the months, his mind had embellished what had happened, creating the torment in his mind that was his beloved sister's demise.

But even his own imaginings hadn't culled that she might have been with child. That those two devils had been jealous enough of a potential bairn that they'd given away her life. He flexed his fists, wishing he had those two bastards in front of him right then and there.

Oh, how he would murder them...

Sarah might not have understood what would have been Thea's fate, but Edward and Ellyson would have been very aware. There wasn't a clan in Scotland that had been untouched by the ravages of the dragoons and the Duke of Cumberland's orders to show no mercy. Men, women, children. It mattered not; they all suffered.

He did not place blame on Sarah. In fact, she'd been

trying to escape her brothers as well, and he'd provided the perfect avenue. As it turned out, his mission to abduct her for revenge had turned into a rescue mission. Some of his guilt assuaged, for he'd not truly intended on harming her. A scare perhaps in being abducted, but never would he have put her through what happened to Thea.

Damn.

He thought back to the lad in the stables at Campbell Castle, so grateful for a little kindness. To the wee lass who said she wanted her mistress back, that her mother needed her, how Thea had meant so much to them. Sarah was right that an entire clan should not have to suffer for the misdeeds of their conniving and selfish leaders.

That was not the type of man he was, to make innocents suffer.

"We should eat before it gets cold," he said, needing to think a lot more before he spoke again.

They ate in silence as his mind ruminated on one plan after another. A number of scenarios played out, but not one seemed more perfect over the other. They could infiltrate the walls and abduct Edward and Ellyson, execute them in the woods. The Shaw clan could appeal to the rest of Clan Chattan, the cooperative confederate between the twelve clans to which the Shaws were a member. He could call upon the other rebel leaders who he'd fought with at Culloden. But the thing was other clans might not want to be involved. The Campbells were massive in size and power. He had to find a way to hit them where it hurt. Which he'd already started by abducting Sarah.

When he'd finished eating, she began to gather their things on the tray, but he stilled her hand. "I'll get it," he offered and took the tray himself to place it outside the door.

"Thank ye," she called out to him.

He stood by the door, his fingers resting on the handle. "Ye're welcome."

Thane felt the heat of her presence before he saw her from the side of his eye, standing by his side. Her fingers brushed his. Tiny flames danced on the skin of his knuckles.

"I'm truly verra verra sorry for your loss, Thane."

He turned to face her, seeing the tears, how much she too was heartbroken, in eyes that were the color of peat. "And I'm verra sorry for yours."

"We have all lost so much in this rebellion," she whispered.

"Shh…" He held his finger to his lips and nodded his head at the empty corridor. "Never know who's listening."

Sarah bit her lip, peering out into the empty corridor. When she leaned back, her arm brushed his, and they both stared down at the spot. "How about we check out the Chamber of Sorrow?" she suggested in a welcome change of subject.

"No' certain that's a very festive thing to do on Christmas morning, but I'm willing to try if ye like."

Sarah shrugged, grimacing slightly. "Better to see what we are fighting for than to sit here wallowing in our grief."

"Excellent point."

Thane took her hand in his, her small, warm fingers sliding comfortably against his. Their palms flattened against one another. He gritted his teeth at the contact and how it sent tiny shivers racing down his spine. As much as touching her excited him, he was also keenly aware of how easy it was to be with her. Thane would have thought it torture, but instead, he was quite calm around her.

Sarah stopped suddenly. "Perhaps ye should leave your weapons here?" Her gaze was on his belt, where a pistol was holstered on one side and a dagger on the other.

"Why would I do that?"

She shrugged. "For the safety of others?"

Thane chuckled at her humor. "I like the way ye think."

Sarah grinned, that impish dimple flashing at him, and he found himself mesmerized for a moment, his gaze tracing the outline of her lips. She looked nothing like her younger brothers. Acted nothing like them, either.

"How are ye possibly related to Edward and Ellyson?" he mused, stopping them in the center of the corridor and glancing down at her.

"They are my brothers," she answered quite literally. "Though Jon and I share a different mother."

"Was their mother unkind?"

Sarah frowned, the crease between her brow tiny, and he had the sudden urge to kiss her there.

"She was not particularly *unkind* to me," she said. "Ignored me mostly. I didna know her well. She died birthing Ellyson. The midwife, after the birth of Edward, warned that she should wait several years, allowing her body to heal after such a traumatic birthing, but she didna wait a month. Not even enough time to be clean in the eyes of the church. I remember her getting my da deep in his cups and having her way with him. She must have conceived that night. Edward and Ellyson are so close in age, less than a year, they could almost be twins."

Thane could not imagine Sarah pulling a trick like that. She just didn't seem the type. "I wonder at her urgency."

Sarah released a long sigh and tugged at his hand, resuming their walk toward the Chamber of Sorrow by way of the tavern common area. "I've speculated on it over the years. She was a cousin of my mother. I think she was desperate to give my da two sons, while my mama had only been able to give him one."

"There are no guarantees. She risked her life when her second child could have been another lass."

"Aye. But jealousy does strange things to people." Sadness edged her words.

He was instantly reminded of her brothers and how they'd left Thea to her fate for their resentful reasons. "Seems it ran in her blood."

"Aye."

They reached the common room, which had taken on a more pleasant odor than before. Bows of holly had been spread near the hearth, ropes of pine on the mantel, and the dogs were gone, as were their messy piles. Platters of currant scones were in the centers of the tables, and jugs of what smelled like cider were beside them.

"Och, but ye've come out," Carrie said. "Have a scone. Cook's specialty on Christmas morn."

"Perhaps after we see your Chamber of Sorrow?" Sarah said. "Unless Tobias, would enjoy one now?"

For a moment, he forgot that she'd renamed him for the sake of their anonymity. Sarah indicated the table to Thane where a steaming pile of scones rested.

"Will they still be here when we come back?" he asked Carrie.

"Of course, and if they're looking to get a bit low, I'll set one aside for ye."

He flashed the woman a grateful smile, working hard to endear themselves to their hosts, so when the Campbells eventually came by, Thane and Sarah would be the last ones from their minds. A happy, jovial couple, versus a villain with an abducted lass, was not likely to be mentioned. "Our thanks."

"We aim to please at Balthazar's." She waved them to follow, leading them back through the various chambers until they reached her own bedchamber. "I keep it back here so no one can sneak in."

⚜

THE DOOR TO THE CHAMBER OF SORROW WAS NOT LOCKED, Sarah noted.

Carrie pushed the door open, which creaked and groaned, revealing a black cavern and swish of air that felt every bit as heavy as Sarah had imagined it would. Their host disappeared into the yawning dark, and Sarah had the intense urge to run. Nothing about this place felt good.

There was a spark as Carrie lit a candle, the flash illuminating her pale, freckled face and the weapons behind her. Several more bursts, and then finally, she brought the chamber to glow, exposing the contents of the room.

And with it, whether real or imagined, the scent of death.

Dawning horror rained down on Sarah, prickling her skin, seizing her throat. When she made a move to enter, her feet remained rooted in place as if her subconscious were fearful of entering. She gripped onto Thane's arm like an anchor, and he led her inside.

"Gathered these up from the battlefield." Carrie swept the candle high, revealing weapons that hung on the plastered walls with crude hooks. "And when others realized what I was doing here, they've brought me more."

A claymore, distinctly a rebel weapon, and above it a musket with a bayonet on the end—dragoon. Here at odds for eternity. They'd at least been cleaned before being put on display.

"Been a few times now. I take the wagon with me." She moved about the room, showing broken arrow shafts, a bow with the string snapped.

An English sword, and another claymore. Sarah studied every weapon for signs of familiarity.

"Is the battlefield close to here?" Sarah asked. If so, she'd ask Thane to take her when the weather dissipated. She wanted to pay respects to the place where her brother had died.

"Och, nay," Carried fluttered her hand as if it weren't a big deal. "Several days ride in the wagon." Her voice had taken on a somber tone. "So many were lost in the battle. This is my shrine to their memory."

Sarah suppressed a shudder as her eyes caught on a Highland cap, the white rosette cockade stained red with blood.

"Did ye lose someone close to ye?" Sarah asked. It was increasingly difficult to conceal her emotions from Carrie, and she was glad for the shadows in the room that hid her expression.

"Aye." But Carrie did not expound on that, and Sarah was afraid of delving too deep.

Afraid she might reveal something about herself and Thane. "I'm verra sorry for your loss," she managed.

Carrie made a non-committal sound but did not return the sentiment. "I'll leave the two of ye alone to mourn. I just ask ye close the door on your way out."

"We will." Sarah took the candleholder from Carrie and stood in the center of the room for several moments before she lifted it high to reveal more of the walls.

Swords, shields, spurs. A pair of roughly used boots. The sleeve of a jacket, the pattern distinctly plaid, and beside it, the sleeve of one that was red. More examples of the battle that waged between two factions. On the floor, beside a table full of coins, rings, and fragments of metal, were two cannonballs. She'd been told that was how Jon had died, torn apart by the blast of a cannon.

Tears came to her eyes, and Sarah wrenched herself away from seeing anymore, running smack into Thane. His arms were around her instantly, holding her tight. His warmth was a comfort she needed. Wanted to bury herself inside.

"This is..." She couldn't even finish her sentence to say how awful the room made her feel.

"Aye," was all he murmured in return, stroking her hair.

Thane took the candle from her, setting it down on the table before she lit his coat on fire.

"This is no' a Chamber of Sorrow," Sarah said. "This is a Chamber of Horrors."

"Do ye want me to destroy it?"

Sarah shook her head, leaning back to look up at him. It felt so good to be in his arms that she didn't want to move away. His face was shadowed like hers, but she could see that he was not jesting.

"As much as I want to say aye, if ye did, we'd both likely be killed. Or cursed."

"Possibly." He tilted his head. "We might be able to escape quickly. The lad out back seemed eager to please."

Sarah smiled. Some of her sorrow ebbed with his teasing. "I'm no' willing to risk your life for a petty thing. But before we leave, I might come in here and steal something. Maybe all of the dragoon items, so no one can mourn them."

"Oh, a thief. Ye have no' mentioned before that ye have the skill."

She shrugged, enjoying the sensation of their arms around each other, and neither seemed inclined to withdraw. "I grew up with three brothers. I learned a few things to survive."

"Do ye recognize anything in here?" He maneuvered them toward the table, his arm still around her waist.

Sarah examined the rings, touching the various items,

imagining who the owners might be. Thankfully, nothing struck her as familiar. "I dinna. What about ye?"

"Nothing," he said quietly.

Sarah glanced up at him. "How many did ye lose?"

"Nearly half our men in the battle. A dozen or more in the retreat. More that were routed out as rebels after." He swallowed hard enough that she could see the lump bob in his throat. "We'll rebuild."

Goodness, they'd lost so many. They were a smaller clan to begin with. But his note of hope filled her with the same sentiment. Though she'd barely known him when his sister had joined her family, now she felt like she'd known him for years, when in reality, less than twenty-four hours had passed.

They had a connection. Mutual loss. Mutual sorrow. And a common goal.

Plus, he'd opened up to her, revealing his strength and integrity. All men should want to be like Thane Shaw.

Without thinking, she leaned up on her tiptoes and pressed her lips to his.

❧ 6 ☙

Thane had not seen this coming. A fantasy or two, sure, but actually kissing Sarah?

Softness and heat pressed against him in body and lips. Desire flooded his veins, and even though he knew he should stop kissing her, he couldn't bring himself to pull away.

With a slant of his head, Thane kissed her deeper. The scent of her surrounded him, and her tiny hands clutched to the front of him, right over the place his heart pounded. He flicked his tongue against her lips, tasting the butter from their breakfast, and then dipping between them when she opened on a gasp.

Tentatively, she touched her tongue to his. Her grip tightened on his shirt, and she let out a little mewl as he stroked his tongue slowly, languidly along hers. She tasted of heaven and sweetness, anything but what he would have thought of someone that should be his enemy.

But he knew she wasn't. That much had been made clear already.

Thane stroked her face, ending the kiss as softly as it had begun, his gaze locked on hers.

"Why did ye do that?" he asked, curious about her motives.

Sarah bit her lip and started to move away, but he held her close. "I'm no' sure. I just...It felt right."

She wasn't wrong. Kissing her had felt very right.

Before the battle at Culloden, he'd been thinking that he needed to take a wife; had flirted with many women, kissed a few. But after the battle, he'd kept everyone at arm's length or longer. No more was his priority to wed, but to keep his clan alive and out of the clutches of the men who would see them all executed for treason.

It had been nearly a year since he'd kissed a lass, and he was certain that any kisses before now had meant little. Why was this one so different? In his gut, he felt that there was something special about this woman. Something to be discovered, once her layers peeled away. And not just her garments, but *her*, the very essence of her.

"I'm...I'm sorry." Sarah shook her head and again tried to pull away. "Ye told me from the beginning that we should be enemies, that I should remember just why we're here together. And I..." She sucked in a breath, pressed her hands to her cheeks, clearly mortified when she needn't have been. "I think the emotion of this room, it—I just could no'—" She broke off then, shaking her head even more.

"Lass, I didna mind the kiss," he soothed, stroking his hand over hers and gently tugging it from her pinkened cheeks. "I would kiss ye again, but no' here. No' in this place of sorrow."

"Horror."

"Both." He took her hand and led her out of the chamber, closing the door behind them as they'd been instructed. Then he guided her back through the common room, nodding to fellow patrons.

Balthazar accosted them along the way, much to Thane's irritation, which he couldn't' show. "Carrie says ye were in her Chamber of Sorrow, and I see it has greatly affected your lass." The man frowned. "Take extra scones with ye back to your room. 'Twill make ye feel better."

That was a ridiculous notion. How were food and drink going to make them feel better when they'd both lost family to a massacre that should never have taken place?

But Thane didn't say that. Instead, he nodded, lifted a tray from a table with at least half a dozen scones on it and a jug of cider. Their host looked ready to balk, but Sarah took that moment to give an all-body shudder, and the old man clamped his lips closed over his rotting teeth.

In their chamber, he poured them each a glass of cider, and they ate the scones sitting on the edge of the bed, each of them trying to absorb all that had happened.

"Balthazar's Tavern may be akin to a type of Hell for me," Sarah said, following a long gulp of cider. So many dreadful and wretched memories flooded her.

"Only parts of it," Thane said. "It would seem our chamber is no' haunted or filled with mad people."

"'Tis true. Unless one of us is mad," she offered with a lift of her shoulders and popped the last of her scone into her mouth.

Thane eyed the tray with four more scones on it. They had been delicious. He could eat the entire tray. But he didn't want to get up, not when it felt so good to be sitting beside her.

"This Christmas is so much different than last." Sarah's shoulders slumped with that admission.

"Oh?" he urged.

"Aye. Last Christmas, Thea decorated the entire great hall with holly and pinecones and sweet-smelling herbs. We had a massive feast, dancing, and games and singing. Thea had a spectacular singing voice. She went to great lengths to make it wonderful for us all." She flashed him a smile.

"That is surprising." Thane pursed his lips in thought. "We didna do all that at Tordarroch Castle. My clan much prefers celebrating the holidays of old. Yule and the winter solstice."

She smiled up at him. "Perhaps that is why she went all out then, because it was so new and magical to her."

"There is something to be said about new traditions." Thane grinned. "Thank ye for sharing your memories of Thea with me."

"'Tis nice to relive them." Her little finger danced over his, where their hands were braced on the edge of the bed. "I'm glad we can share them together."

"Me too." And then, before he could change his mind, Thane bent to kiss her once more.

⁂

SARAH WAS PLAYING WITH FIRE.

Already she'd crossed too many lines. Her brothers would have her head if they knew she was behaving this way. Kissing a man she barely knew in a chamber they were meant to share for the night. A man she'd willingly allowed to abduct her. If they'd knew she'd packed the bag before he'd ever arrived—Lord, but they would kill her.

And she'd be fine with it, for she'd had a chance to feel Thane's lips on hers. A man worthy of a kiss. A man worthy of so much more.

Their fingers entwined, his thumb brushing over her

knuckles. What would it be like to kiss him every day like this? To glory in the soft sweep of his lips, the sensual stroke of his tongue?

That was when the idea came to her. She needed to be ruined. And who better for the task than Thane? Should her brothers catch up to them, it would make it impossible for her to partner with anyone else. Whoever they sold her to would not pay for a woman who'd already been claimed by another.

But Thane...He was honorable. Felt guilty at having abducted her. Even the tough attitude he tried to have with her was seen through easily enough. The man was formidable when he needed to be and in the next breath filled with heart. Much like his sister had been. Which meant that he would not simply steal her virginity if she asked him, too. She'd have to *make* him take it.

Sarah threaded her free hand in his hair, kissing him deeper, and he enjoyed it, judging from the sound in the back of his throat. She had no practice at wooing or seducing. Though Thane was not the first man she'd ever kissed, she'd done nothing more than that. And the only knowledge she had of what happened between a man and a woman was what she'd overheard the maids talking about after a feast that had seen plenty of them deep in their cups. But from what she'd heard, she thought she could piece together a fairly decent seduction.

And she'd not know until she tried.

With that in mind, and the confidence of someone well versed in lovemaking, she lifted herself up and straddled Thane's lap. The crux of her thighs pressed to the hardened length of him, sending a shudder of pleasure through her.

Oh, my...The maids had not been jesting about that part. Frissons of wicked decadence raced through her, and when she rubbed herself back and forth, yet more intense quivers followed.

No wonder they did this. It actually felt rather good. Better than good. Not the stories she'd been told as a girl by her da. That to rut with a lad would only lead to unbearable pain and was best saved for marriage, when the blessing of God would lessen the torment.

Da was wrong, it would seem. Or he'd lied.

Thane's hands came around her backside, gripping her arse and massaging, and he too moved beneath her, increasing the friction as his arousal stroked against hers. She moaned against his mouth, a little surprised at the sounds she was making. Then he was flipping her around so her back was flush to the mattress, and he was over her, between her thighs.

He kissed her harder, with more vigor and passion, tossing all her sensations into the air like fairy dust until she felt like she was in a magical dream. His hand swept up her ribs, clutching at her breast, and then he tore his mouth from hers and traveled heatedly over her neck and downward until his lips clamped over her nipple.

Sarah cried out at that, bucking upward. *Goodness...*She'd not thought touching could feel any better, but it just kept getting more intense and more pleasurable.

"Dear God, I love the way ye respond," he said, panting, his eyes on her. Desire filled his gaze, made his eyelids dip.

Sarah grinned encouragingly. This was going quite well. "Your touch is magic."

He kissed her again, caressing her everywhere until she was floating in a sea of delicious awareness she never wanted to be rescued from.

"I want ye," he groaned against her lips.

His words, spoken so passionately, pinged off all the right spots in her mind and body.

Seduction had been so easy. And so exciting. "Ye can have me. I give myself willingly."

There, she'd said it. And soon she would be ruined, and it would be wonderful.

Thane pushed her skirts up, fumbled with his breeches, and then she felt the very heat of him at her core.

"Are ye certain?" he asked, gaze locked on hers, eyes filled with question.

"Aye," she said with a confidence she'd never felt so keenly before.

Thane let out a satisfied groan and surged forward, the invasion accompanied by a sharp clamp of pain. Sarah cried out unbidden at the ache, surprised that it should have felt that way when everything else had been so wonderful.

Thane stilled, letting out a curse, the force of which blew the hair from her forehead. Sarah's eyes had been clamped closed, but his angry tone made her snap open her lids.

"Ye were a virgin," he accused, a thunderstorm clouding his expression. Gone was the heady look of his lowered lids.

Tears sprang to her eyes. "Aye," she whispered.

"Why did ye no' bloody tell me?"

Sarah swallowed hard. Perhaps tricking him into taking her virginity had been stupid, but she had given her full permission. "I did no' think it mattered. I consented."

Thane cursed, withdrawing from her body, leaving her feeling empty and lost. She reached for him as he climbed off, but he backed away from the bed and shoved himself back into his breeches. "I would no' have done that. 'Tis no' honorable."

Exactly as she'd imagined he would act if he'd known. Tears fell in earnest now, hot waves down her cheeks. "It was no' your choice to make." She shoved her skirts back down, pulling her legs up tight to her chest, aching all the more.

"Why?" There was true anguish in his tone.

"Because if my brothers come for me, and they *will*, I can be of no use to them if I am spoiled. I dinna want to be their pawn."

"But why would ye have me be the one to spoil ye?" He pressed his fist to his chest.

Without hesitation, she answered, "Because ye're so honorable. A good man."

"And so ye wished to trick me into marriage then?"

She shook her head vigorously, everything spinning out of control. That had been the last thing on her mind. And she hated the way his anger had turned to pain. "Nay, I thought... If I were to ruin myself, I'd want to do with it a man like ye, rather than just anyone."

All the anger dissipated from him now, his shoulders sagging, and he trudged back toward her. Thane sighed and sat down on the bed next to her, gathering her in his arms. He was quiet for a long time, and she remained very still. Afraid if he remembered that he was holding her, he'd walk away. "If I had known, I would have taken my time. Made sure ye were ready."

"I am ready."

"I mean, your body."

"Oh." She sucked in a weary breath and stared up at him, meeting his gaze head-on, wanting him to see the truth in her eyes. "I was no' trying to trick ye, I swear. I dinna seek marriage. I only sought to rid myself of the bargaining chip my brothers are trying to sell."

Thane stroked her hair, wiped away her tears. The pain in his expression receded and returned the man she'd fallen for. Oh, dear heavens...Aye, she had fallen for him. Swept up and deposited right on the shores of his affection, should he want her.

"I will marry ye." Conviction powered each syllable.

"What?" She pushed away from him then. Had he not understood her? "I told ye that's no' what I seek."

"I know, lass. But it is the only way to make certain they canna sell ye. Your brothers will lie about your virginity for the riches it will bring them. I'll protect ye because I was no' able to protect my sister."

Sarah glanced down at the rug on the dirt floor. "I canna ask ye to do that." Keeping her safe wouldn't bring Thea back, and she didn't want him to feel obligated to her for the rest of their lives. For eternity.

"Ye didna." He tipped her chin up. "I offered. Of my own free will, I consent." He pressed his lips to hers softly. Saints, but it felt so good. "Besides, I like the idea of being able to kiss ye more."

"Truly?" His embrace was warm, comforting, and she felt safe with him, cared for.

"Aye." He kissed her again and then left the bed once more, though this time he only went to the basin where he took a loose rag and dipped it in water.

She watched, curious, as he came back to her and then gentle as he could washed between her legs. His ministrations were perhaps the most considerate of any she'd ever had.

"To soothe the ache," he murmured.

"Thank ye," she said.

"If ye'll still have me...I'd like to finish what we started, only make it better this time."

Tentatively, she nodded. But then she knew he'd want to hear her say it aloud. "Ye have my permission to make love to me."

And then he was laying her back down on the bed, and

once more she was melting into the sheets and sighing with pleasure. He kissed his way down the length of her body until he hovered over the very center of her.

"I want to kiss ye here."

"That is…" That had not been discussed by the maids. "It sounds…"

But she couldn't find the words, and it didn't matter anyway because he robbed her of all sense as his tongue stroked the sensitive folds of her sex. Again and again, he stroked until she was clutching at the sheets and crying out in pleasure. Wave after delicious heady wave crashed over her. *Oh my*…Thane was a skilled lover. Made her feel powerful one moment and weak in the knees the next. And pleasure, there was so much of it.

"That was what I meant before," he said, crawling up the length of her still-shuddering body. "Now, ye're ready."

This time when he pushed inside her, there was no pain, only more pleasure. She gasped, letting the last vestiges of control go. Wrapping herself around him, she followed his lead, kissed his shoulders, his mouth. Gripped his arse, stroked his back. Cried out when he somehow made her body break apart once more and drank in the sounds of his rapture as he whispered her name over and over again.

"Ye're mine forever now, lass," he said, nuzzling against her neck before meeting her gaze. There was not even an inkling of regret in his words or eyes.

Sarah grinned, placing her arms around his neck and threading her fingers into his hair. "Who knew revenge and abduction could be so…satisfying?"

Thane let out a roar of laughter and gently bit her lip. "*Ye* are satisfying."

They lay in bliss for an hour or so, whispering, touching and eating the rest of the scones. This was the first time Thane had ever done this with a woman. Just lying there languidly sharing stories from their childhood. Their likes and dislikes. Exploring one another, both in mind and body.

In the span of an hour, he'd learned more about Sarah than he knew about any other person—even his twin sister Thea.

Sarah was ticklish behind her knees and at her ankles, but not on her ribs. She loved sunrise more than sunset, and her favorite time of year was in spring when dewdrops dripped from trees onto the tip of her tongue. The lass had a penchant for sweets and disliked spirits, but she'd drink them if she must and agreed to taste the whisky he distilled himself at Tordarroch.

They'd both learned to play the lute when they were young, but he was the only one who'd continued to play. He told her about how he and Thea would combine their musical talents to entertain the clan, to which Sarah belted out in the most angelic voice he'd ever heard a ballad of winter and the spring that was to come.

When they were willing to brave the cold, they pulled on their cloaks on the pretense of checking on the horses, but in reality, it was to check the weather.

The crowd in the common area had slimmed now that the scones were gone. In the corner, an older man sung and played his lute. The brim of his hat pulled low, casting a shadow on his face. The two of them were very tempted to join him, but at that moment, Balthazar came barreling into the room, demanding the man change his Christmas tune to one of battle.

Rather than brave the kitchens and more of Cook's ladle flinging, they went out the front door, the cold of winter slapping against their cheeks, along with a gust that brought with it dustings of snow from the ground. They slammed the door shut to keep it from entering the tavern, though it was likely too late.

The snow was easily above their ankles, but the lads had shoveled a path leading from the front door around the back of the tavern toward the stable.

"Still coming down," Thane mused.

"Aye, but at least the sky is not only white with clouds. A bit of blue peeking through the white means we may yet get a reprieve." The wind whipped against them, and Sarah tripped then clutched at his arm to keep from falling. And good thing, because right then, a massive icicle fell from the thatched roof, stabbing into the snow where she'd just been. Both of them leapt back, he as though to protect her and she because her life was flashing before her eyes.

"We'll need a good two or three days reprieve if we're to make it back in decent time. Might have to stop along the way at another tavern or two."

"Additional adventures then." She grinned up at him, excitement in the creases about her eyes. What had transpired between the two of them was almost enough to erase the reasons they'd got together to begin with. Almost.

"Aye, but also more possibility of your brothers finding us," he reminded her grimly.

The light left her eyes then, and she seemed to remember that she'd been running from them suddenly. "Do ye think they've left yet?"

Thane nodded. "They'd no' wait too long to come after ye. And our tracks may yet be visible in the snow, though with the way it fell through the night, I'm hoping most were covered. At any rate, they'll have lost us by the time they get to the road, given all the others who've traversed."

"But they would guess it was ye?" She glanced around nervously as if expecting to see her brothers leap out.

"Does your clan have any other enemies?" That was a silly question, and he knew it.

"Of course."

"Then maybe we have a chance yet." He offered that as hope.

Sarah shivered, and he took her hand, looping her arm in his and rubbing vigorously at the exposed skin of her fingers. They made their way to the stables and poked their heads inside when no lads were seen lurking about.

The stable was long and smoky, with the telltale sounds of horse snuffling and stomping.

"Destiny, we've come to greet ye," Thane called out, and his horse stuck his head out from one of the stalls, letting out a hearty neigh.

They made their way down until they reached him, observing a clean stall, a bucket of water and another filled with hay.

"I see ye're being properly spoiled." Thane stroked his hand over his horse's soft muzzle.

"Why did ye name him Destiny?" Sarah asked.

"I found him on the battlefield. Or rather, he found me." He'd never told anyone this story before, but with Sarah, it came out easily. He would need to keep some of the details vague, so if anyone were listening in, they wouldn't realize which side he fought on. He also kept to himself that Destiny's previous master had been a dragoon, evident from the contents he found in the attached satchel, and the crest stamped into the saddle. Wasn't it ironic that the horse of his enemy had saved his life?

"This is going to be intriguing," Sarah said, wiggling her brows.

"The enemy was surrounding me, knocking me back. My own horse had already been massacred, and so I was on foot, in danger of joining my brethren in the beyond. Then from behind me comes this massive warhorse. He nuzzles me in the back as men advance on me, taking aim. I leapt up into the saddle, and he took off, with shots fired at us from behind. He saved my life, and the fact that we found each other on the field like that, well, it felt like Destiny."

Sarah leaned against him, her hand joining his in stroking the horse. "That is an incredible story. And the perfect name. I'm glad for my sake that he found ye."

Thane grinned. "He's a good horse. And for that reason, he should be spoiled for the rest of his days."

৩%৩

SARAH LEANED HER HEAD AGAINST THANE'S SHOULDER, SO glad that he'd come to Campbell lands. Even if his intent had been to abduct her, which now seemed like a massive jest.

He'd rescued her from a fate that could have been horrible. And to think she was now going to be linked to her dearest friend's brother—a man of honor and integrity—she couldn't have dreamed up a better scenario.

They left the stable, agreeing to spend one more night at the tavern, and then hopefully be on their way the following morning.

By the time they made it back to their chamber, the delicious stew they'd been smelling all day waited for them on the table, along with wine and thick brown bread. They ate with gusto, having worked up an appetite earlier in the day, and when their meal was complete, they made love again and again.

When morning finally broke, a slim crack of light was seen through where the wall met the roof, and so they rose with tired eyes. Sarah prayed the weather had waned, and they could be on their way from this tavern of sorrow. And yet, she'd always remember it fondly for being the place where she'd given herself to Thane.

"That sun is a good sign." Thane climbed from the bed, giving her arse a gentle pat.

Sarah giggled and rolled over. "Ye think we can leave?"

"Aye, we can try." He tugged back the covers, and she squealed at the cold blast of air.

They dressed quickly and exited the chamber, skipping the porridge in favor of a hunk of bread with butter, and then before the sun had fully risen, they climbed onto Destiny's back and took off at a trot down the road. Some of the snow had started to melt, and with the morning sun the twinkling white moors took on more of a glistening shine.

Just as they had the night they escaped Campbell Castle, they stopped every few hours to rest Destiny and relieve themselves. They packed their canteen with snow to keep it full. No one seemed to be following them, and indeed they did not pass anyone of note on the road.

In the distance, the clanging of kirk bells could be heard coming from a small village.

"I think we need to make it official," Thane said.

"What's that?" Sarah mused sleepily.

"Our union. Would ye, Sarah Campbell, consent to being my wife?"

She sat up a little straighter, nodding as she looked into his quite serious gaze. Though she'd agreed before, the fact that he asked her once more warmed her heart. "Every day for the rest of my life."

They rode into the village and to the kirk, where they found a priest more than willing to wed them for a small fortune.

"I dinna have a ring for ye." Thane frowned as they stood on the stairs out front of the kirk.

"Wait," she said. "I have one."

Sarah pulled the small box from her satchel, revealing the ring that had once been her mother's. The rubies glistened in the sunlight. "My ma gave me this. 'Twas hers."

"'Tis perfect, just like ye."

Sarah's face heated at his words. He made her feel so special. She passed the jewelry box to Thane, and when it came time to place the ring on her finger, he did so slowly, eyes locked on hers. So much emotion was conveyed there, so much trust, and anticipation.

They were in this together. Them against the injustices of the world.

She couldn't help but smile with joy, for even though destiny had brought them together, it would seem the two of them had forged their own path from there on.

When the priest said the groom could kiss his bride,

Sarah didn't wait. She tossed herself into his arms and pressed her lips to his, startling the priest and their witnesses by her boldness. But Thane was not surprised at all. By the way he wrapped his arms around her, she knew he relished her.

"That's my lass," Thane said with a chuckle.

They left the kirk and took a room in the village tavern. Regaled by singing and festive games, which they joined in this time, not feeling threatened or haunted, but amid company they could revel in. They feasted on roasted pheasant and stewed turnips in a thick brown sauce that was perfect for dipping bread into. And that night, when Thane made love to her, Sarah felt a deep emotion for him all the way to her soul...

Love. Wholly and passionately. Everything tingled inside and out, and not just from his touch, but his gaze, his presence, the idea of a future together.

As they lay in the dark, fingers and legs entwined, their breaths in sync, she whispered, "I love ye."

Thane rolled toward her, tugging her close against him. "I love ye, too, lass. I canna believe that I set out to steal ye, and instead, ye've stolen my heart."

EPILOGUE

Several months later...

The prisoners arrived just before sunset, shackled on top of their mounts, shackled and gagged, so no one had to hear them speak.

"They are here," Sarah said quietly. Her eyes were riveted on the two men who'd been willing to sell her. The two men who had been responsible for Thane's sister's death.

"We dinna have to go through with this." Thane tucked his arm around her shoulders. She was beautiful in winter, but even more so in spring. Especially with his bairn rounding out her belly. Sarah had taken to the Shaw clan as if she'd been a member all along. They loved her dearly, and she loved them. "There is always an execution or exile. I can put them on a ship to the Americas."

She shook her head. "I canna have the guilt of their deaths on my conscience or the guilt for it being on yours. Nor do I want to unleash them on anyone else."

Thane cupped her chin, brushed his lips over hers. "I will do whatever ye want, my love."

"Your plans for their imprisonment are perfect. Perhaps in time, they will be reformed and can be set free. But for now, they will be punished." Sarah wrapped her arms around his middle and tucked her body close to his. "Thank ye for all ye've done."

"I couldna have done it without ye." And that was the truth. They'd worked as a team from Christmas Eve until now, securing the safety of the Campbell clan, and the men responsible for Thea's death, and it had been glorious. "Both our clans will thrive from here on out."

Hand in hand, they met Angus Campbell, the new Campbell laird, outside Tordarroch gates, eyeing Edward and Ellyson, who glared down at them.

"Thank ye, Angus." Sarah embraced her uncle. "The clan will be in excellent hands with ye."

"Nay lass, thank ye, and your husband." Her uncle glanced down at her rounded belly. "And I see we may yet have an heir to Jon's seat growing in your womb."

Sarah pressed her hand over her middle. "We would be honored for our child to have such a choice."

"Your father would want that."

Angus nodded to Thane and reached out his hand, grasping Thane's arm and shaking it. "We owe ye a great debt."

"Ye owe me nothing, I did my duty." And he meant it.

Sarah, Thane and Angus made a deal, surreptitiously. A coup, really. With Thane and Sarah's assistance, Angus had been able to take over his clan. A task which had not been too hard, given how everyone had felt about Edward and Ellyson's rule. Not to mention they did not want a war on their head, which Thane might have exaggerated slightly, with the help of his Chattan clan confederate.

"Ye'll make an excellent leader," Sarah said. "My da and Jon would be so proud of ye."

Angus was Sarah's uncle, the much younger brother of her father, and the natural and best choice for the clan's new rule. He'd graciously accepted the appointment after a secret vote by the elders. Part of the plan was that Edward and Ellyson would be brought to Shaw lands, where they would be held prisoner for the remainder of their days, unless it was deemed safe for them to be let out. Sarah did not want to execute her brothers, though they deserved it. And Thane wanted to make her happy. He supposed death in this case would not make right what had been done in the past. Thea wasn't coming back. But at least they could honor her memory every day in having freed the Campbells from the rotten brothers' rule.

"Will ye join us for supper, Uncle?" Sarah asked.

"Gladly." Angus offered Sarah his arm, and they walked into Tordarroch ahead of Thane, who waited behind to escort his prisoners to their new quarters.

When Sarah was out of earshot, Thane turned on the two bastard brothers. "I'm going to make your lives a living hell, lads. Ye took my sister and possibly her child from this world without a care. My wife has seen fit to let ye live because she is a merciful and good woman. But that does no' mean ye get to live free and well."

Thane dragged the shackled men to the dungeon of Tordarroch and grinned widely. In the end, he'd gotten more than he bargained for, retribution, love and a bigger family. Glancing down at the two men who glared fire and hate at him, Thane said, "Welcome home. I like to call this the Chamber of Sorrow."

DON'T MISS OUT ON ELIZA KNIGHT'S NEW AND EXCITING series — Prince Charlie's Angels, starting with Book One: *The Rebel Wears Plaid*!

THESE HEROINES RISK THEIR LIVES TO PROTECT Jacobite soldiers. Hiding them, healing their wounds, and aiding in their escape from enemy forces, puts these fiery ladies in harm's way, but their loyalty wins out over fear every time.

TORAN FRASER IS HELL-BENT ON TAKING DOWN THE Jacobites. On a late-night mission, he's intercepted by a woman known only as "Mistress J" who's determined to put Prince Charlie back on the throne of Scotland. Toran can't resist her appeal—especially with her pistol pointed at his heart—and suddenly finds himself joining the rebellion...

BY DAY, HIGHBORN JENNY MACKINTOSH RUNS HER ESTATE in the Highlands. By night, she raises coin, delivers weapons, and recruits soldiers for the Jacobite rebellion. When she encounters a handsome Highlander who is clearly on the run, she is more than a little intrigued. She isn't expecting to become the target of his sworn enemy...

"THE REBEL WEARS PLAID IS FABULOUS—BOLD, adventurous, and brimming with intrigue and memorable characters."--Cathy Maxwell, New York Times bestselling author

. . .

"AN ADMIRABLY COURAGEOUS HEROINE, A WONDERFULLY hot hero, impeccable history, well-crafted characters, and edge-of-your-seat adventure makes this Highland romance irresistible. An excellent beginning to an engrossing series. I can't wait for the next one!" --*New York Times* bestselling author Jennifer Ashley

"*OUTLANDER* FANS WILL BE THRILLED BY ELIZA KNIGHT'S perfect mix of history and romance."—Jennifer McQuiston, *New York Times* bestselling author

"THE INTRIGUE AND HISTORICAL DETAILS ARE CAPTIVATING, but readers should be prepared for an excruciatingly slow burn in the love story, which remains relatively understated for a large chunk of the novel. Fans of strong female protagonists and subtle passion will be pleased." --*Publisher's Weekly*

ABOUT THE AUTHOR

Eliza (E.) Knight is an award-winning and *USA Today* best-selling author of over fifty sizzling historical romance and rip-your-heart-out historical fiction. While not reading, writing or researching for her latest book, she chases after her three children. In her spare time (if there is such a thing...) she likes daydreaming, wine-tasting, traveling, hiking, staring at the stars, watching movies, shopping and visiting with family and friends. She lives atop a small mountain with her own knight in shining armor, three princesses and two very naughty puppies. Visit Eliza at http://www.elizaknight.com or her historical blog History Undressed: www.historyun-dressed.com. Sign up for her newsletter to get news about books, events, contests and sneak peaks! http://eepurl.com/CSFFD

facebook.com/elizaknightfiction

twitter.com/elizaknight

instagram.com/elizaknightfiction

bookbub.com/authors/eliza-knight

goodreads.com/elizaknight

www.ingramcontent.com/pod-product-compliance
Lightning Source LLC
Chambersburg PA
CBHW070917160726
48004CB00003B/1410